NOTHING IS GOING RIGHT FOR RORY!

Margie brushed crumbs off her hands. "Let's go in the living room to study."

Oh no, thought Rory. Everything in that room was *really* falling apart. She pulled Margie aside. "Margie," she whispered. "Don't take her in that room. Everything in there is old and worn out."

"Aw, come on, Rory. She won't care," said Margie as she joined Jennifer.

They filed into the living room. Rory tried to steer them away from the couch. "Why don't we sprawl out on the floor?" she asked.

"This is fine," replied Jennifer as she sat down on the checkered sofa. The springs gave in. She sat down . . . down . . . down . . . bottom to the floor, feet high in the air.

"*UGH!* Get me out of here!" Jennifer's high-pitched screech could be heard throughout the house.

My Life Is Going to the Dogs

HELP!

My Life Is Going to the Dogs

Elizabeth Koehler-Pentacoff

Text copyright © 1997 by Elizabeth Koehler-Pentacoff.

Published by Troll Communications L.L.C.

Cover art by S. D. Schindler

Printed in the United States of America.

10 9 8 7 6 5 4 3 2 1

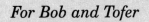

For Bob and Tofer

CHAPTER

1

"Hey, Rory," said Margie. "Let's sit up front."

"No," Rory answered, sliding behind a desk near the back of the classroom. "I want to sit here."

"Why?" asked Margie.

Rory shrugged. She didn't want to explain in front of the other kids. Margie looked puzzled but sat next to her, anyway. Suddenly the door banged open. Chris Nyberg charged into the room.

"Hey, Maddening Mueller!" he yelled to Rory. She shuddered as he plopped into the desk directly in front of her. *Chris* would *have to sit there,* she thought. *What a way to start off the school year.*

"Creep-show Chris!" Rory sassed back.

He was the ultimate class creep. Everything about him irked her. Chris always wore his hair just long enough to look like he was in bad need of a haircut. He didn't just come into a room—he clunked into it as if he wanted to make enough racket so everyone would look at him. Even his walk was irritating.

"Rory, Rory, Hallelujah," he sang.

"Oh, Chris, get a life," said Margie.

Good old Margie. She's a terrific best friend, Rory thought. She might not understand why Rory needed to sit in the back of the room, but she'd stick by Rory through anything. Even through Chris's obnoxious remarks.

"Hey, want to go skateboarding in the park after school?" asked Margie.

Rory nodded. She and Margie did everything together. They rode bikes, did art projects, and played with Rory's dog nearly every day.

She watched Margie take out her looseleaf binder.

"Reading, math, science," said Barb, the girl who sat behind Margie. "Wow, Margie. You've got them all labeled already?"

Margie flipped to the section in her binder marked NOTES. "It's just a habit I have. I like to be organized."

"That's why you get straight A's and I don't," said Rory.

Even though they were best friends and did a lot of the same things, Rory and Margie were very different. Rory's daydreaming hurt her grades. She was lucky to earn B's and C's because she just couldn't keep her mind on her work.

Already Rory was imagining her favorite fantasy. She pretended that her parents were engineers or doctors. They lived in a fancy house with a pool, and Rory could wear all the coolest clothes.

Rory smoothed the collar of her dress. Usually she and Margie sat up front, but today Rory didn't want anyone to look at her too carefully.

Times had been hard for Rory and her family ever since her father's hours were cut at the factory last spring. The Muellers were never really rich, but at least they'd always had money for new back-to-school clothes.

All summer Rory wore clothes her mom had made, but for the first day of school, Rory wanted to wear something "bought."

Rory gazed at Margie's new school clothes longingly.

A week before school started, she had begged her mom, "Can't we go to the mall and buy just one dress? Please?"

Her mom had sighed. "Rory, we don't have money for that right now."

She remembered picking at the worn Formica on the kitchen table as she heard her mother's disappointing answer.

"Well, I guess we could try the thrift shop," added her mother. "We might be able to find something there."

Rory was surprised to see a cute blue dress hanging in the store's window, which turned out to be just her size. So Rory got the outfit, but she still longed for a new dress. She just didn't look as smart as Margie did in her brand-new, back-to-school skirt and blouse.

Rory pulled out a piece of paper and a pencil from her desk. She hoped this year's teacher would be nicer than Mrs. Irving had been last year. In fourth grade, whenever Rory would start to daydream, Mrs. Irving always made her stay in at recess and write "I will pay attention in class" one hundred times. Although Rory's hand would get stiff and sore, the punishment never really did any good. The next day, Rory's mind would wander into fantasyland all over again.

"Good morning," said the fifth-grade teacher. She smiled at the class as the last few kids straggled into the classroom.

"Hi," said Rory and Margie in unison.

Rory watched the teacher write her name on the board. "I'm Ms. Bellini," she said. "But you can call me Ms. B."

Well, at least her handwriting is a little messy, thought Rory. Not perfect like Mrs. Irving's. Mrs. Irving always made them write their assignments over again if so much as a few t's were crossed too high or too low.

"All right, class. Everyone find a seat," said Ms. B. "I need to take roll."

At that moment, Jennifer Thompson flounced into the room. She had moved to the Lincoln Elementary area over the summer, and she lived only a few blocks from Rory and Margie. They had already met at the park.

"Hi, Jennifer," said Margie. "I like your jeans."

Rory stared at them. She knew they were expensive.

"Oh, these old things?" Jennifer said as she slid into the seat in front of Margie.

The class quieted as Ms. B. read the names. "Alison?"

"Here."

"Christopher?"

The class giggled at the formality of his name.

"Yo," said Chris smartly. "But call me Chris."

"Creep-show Chris," muttered Rory to herself.

"Aurora," said Ms. B.

"Here," answered Rory.

"Hey, Aurora," whispered Chris as he turned around to face her. "Sleeping Beauty," he taunted.

Darn, thought Rory. He called her that irritating nickname whenever Mrs. Irving had caught Rory daydreaming last year. Aurora was Rory's full name—and also the name of the main character in "Sleeping Beauty." And Chris thought he was oh-so-clever.

Chris leaned *waaay* back in his chair. *TAP. TAP.* The chair hit Rory's desk. *TAP TAP TAP.*

Rory groaned. Chris grinned. She hoped Ms. B. would move him somewhere else.

"At my old school, all the boys were so much nicer—and cuter," Jennifer whispered to Margie, tossing back her golden curls. Rory wished she could be confident like Jennifer, but she acted so superior it was sickening.

Margie leaned forward. "What school did you go to last year?" she asked.

"Amelia Earhart Elementary," said Jennifer. "It's a private school." She looked at Rory. "My dad's a doctor, you know. And my mom's a lawyer."

"Amelia Earhart?" asked Chris. "Too bad you don't just fly away."

Rory held back a smile. She secretly wished Jennifer would fly away, too. Over the past few weeks, Jennifer and Margie had become very friendly.

The morning flew by as Ms. B. passed out books and reviewed class rules. Rory finished copying the class schedule just as the bell rang for recess.

Rory and Margie decided to sit at one of the picnic tables. Some of the other fifth-graders stood nearby. Rory heard giggling and whispering. As she turned to see what was going on, she saw Chris staring at her.

"What do *you* want?" Rory asked him.

"I want to see your label," he said, smirking.

At that comment, Jennifer and the girls around her laughed.

"What do you mean?" asked Rory.

One of the group, Barb, turned to her. "Jennifer says you're wearing *her* dress."

"*Her* dress?" asked Margie. "How could it be *her* dress?"

Suddenly Barb leaned over and reached for the back of Rory's outfit.

She pulled out the label.

"Hey—it says *JT*," said Barb.

"See," said Jennifer smugly. "Those are my initials."

Everyone but Margie crowded around Rory, peering to see.

"My mom gave this dress to Goodwill," said Jennifer just as the bell rang. "I wore it last year."

Rory jerked away. She wanted to die. She felt a million eyes on her as she walked back into the room.

CHAPTER

2

Rory unsnapped Charlie's leash. It had been a nice walk. Whenever she spent time with her terrier, somehow she was able to forget about her old clothes, Chris's teasing, and Jennifer's snobbishness.

Rory hadn't seen any of her classmates after school, and there weren't any cats or squirrels to tempt Charlie into a chase.

She remembered the time the Wilsons' cat had had kittens under their porch. They locked Charlie in the basement, but he still howled all day because those cats were in *his* yard.

By dinnertime he had pushed and scratched at the basement window until the latch opened. When he escaped he ran to the front porch just in time to see the cat run off toward town. Rory had been helping her mom weed the yard when she saw him. The two of them set out to chase Charlie. They had run up and down the block, around the house, over the hedges, and through Johnson's Creek until Charlie decided he'd given them enough exercise. He'd slept in Rory's room ever since that night.

Rory opened the screen door. "Mom, Dad. We're home." She walked into the kitchen to wash her hands.

"Remember Charlie's vitamins?" asked her mother, taking the pins out of her mouth that she was using to hem Mrs. Koenig's flowered skirt. Rory giggled. Her dad was standing on a chair, wearing the skirt.

He hammed it up, making his voice squeaky and high. "Oh, darling. Don't you love my new outfit?"

Rory played along. "Absolutely. You look *maaarvelous* in flowers!"

Charlie sat patiently by the refrigerator, waiting for his treat.

Rory took a slice of cheese and wrapped it around one of the pills.

"Here, Charlie," she said. He took it happily and ran into the living room.

"Good boy," said Rory.

"That was easy," commented her mother. She put her sewing box away and went down the hall. Rory's dad removed the skirt and started to set the table.

"I'm surprised he didn't put up more of a fight," he said as he took out the napkins.

"Charlie likes cheese," Rory said, placing silverware on the table.

Mrs. Mueller came back into the kitchen. "How was school today?" she asked. "Did the new dress work out?"

"Yeah," Rory mumbled. Her mother had enough on her mind. She didn't need to worry about Rory's problems.

Thank goodness tomorrow isn't a school day, she thought. Maybe Jennifer and Chris would get tired of picking on her. Or maybe she'd think of something clever to say back to them.

"Glad Charlie didn't give you any trouble on your walk," said her father. "Last week I took him to the park, and he caught sight of a squirrel in a tree. He got so excited, he nearly climbed up after it."

Rory smiled at her father's story. "Charlie's always a good boy for me," she said. *At least something had gone right today,* she thought.

CHAPTER

3

On Saturday, Rory and her mother stood in line at the Pantry. Once a week, the Pantry passed out cheese and canned goods for the needy.

Rory had to go along with her mother to help carry everything home. Arms laden with bags, they would walk to the bus stop in silence. She always prayed no one from school would see her. Rory hated these mornings.

As they stood in line, Rory tried to cover her face with the bags—just in case someone passed by.

She looked at the old woman in front of her. She was dressed in a worn coat and was pushing a shopping cart. It was filled with her belongings. The woman smiled at Rory. Two of her front teeth were missing. Shyly, Rory smiled back.

What happened to her? Rory wondered. What happened to her home? Didn't she have a family to take care of her? When she saw the old sleeping bag in the cart, Rory realized that the woman slept outside in the cold. For a moment, Rory felt thankful. At least she had a family and a home.

But the moment passed as Rory stared at the moving cars. She saw a familiar face. Jennifer? It couldn't be! Quickly Rory looked away. But it was too late.

Jennifer's mother's Mercedes had stopped at a red light. Jennifer stuck her head out of the car window. "Rory, what *are* you doing?"

Rory was speechless. What could she say? Maybe she should just ignore her and the light would turn green.

Rory stepped behind her mom and faced the opposite direction.

"Rory!" Jennifer yelled again.

"Rory," said her mother. "Aren't you going to say hello?" Mrs. Mueller waved to Jennifer and her mom.

The car pulled over to the curb. Jennifer's mother opened the door and got out. "Would you like a ride?"

Rory felt her face get hot.

"Sure," shouted her mother. "But we're not done yet."

"It's all right," said Jennifer's mother. "We're not in a hurry."

Rory wanted to die. The wait for the free food seemed longer than ever, even though they were only third in line.

By the time they had their bags, Rory's hands were sweaty.

How could she face the ride home with Miss Stuck-up? Worse yet, what if Jennifer told everyone at school about Rory taking handouts?

Jennifer jumped out of the car. "May I help you, Mrs. Mueller?" She grabbed the bags from Rory's mom and carried them to the trunk.

"Why, thank you," said Mrs. Mueller.

Jennifer's mother opened the trunk. "We'll do a little shuffling," she explained as she stuffed department store bags together to make room for the groceries. "We did a little shopping today. Jennifer needed some more back-to-school clothes."

Right, thought Rory. *To replace the stuff she gave to the thrift shop.* She glanced in one bag. The price tag hung from a sweater. The price of the sweater was almost as much as her dad made in a week at the factory.

"It's nice to see you both again," said Rory's mother, once they were on their way. "I do love your car." She caressed the seat with her hand. "This leather upholstery is beautiful."

"I like my dad's Porsche better," interrupted Jennifer, glancing back at Rory. "I get it when I'm sixteen."

"A Porsche?" exclaimed Rory's mother. "What a lucky girl. I've always dreamed of owning one."

This is just great, thought Rory. Why did her mom have to gush?

Finally Jennifer's mother pulled into their graveled driveway. Rory opened the door and jumped out as quickly as she could.

"Thanks," she mumbled to Jennifer's mother as she ran into the house.

"Wait," called Rory's mother. "Help me carry the food!"

Rory wished she could disappear. She turned and trudged back to the car. Jennifer's eyes were on her.

"See you in school," said Jennifer sweetly.

"Sure," said Rory, grabbing some bags and stumbling up the driveway.

After they were safely in the house, Rory buried her face into her hands. "Now what am I going to do?"

Her mother put her arm around Rory's shoulders. "It's all right, honey."

"But how can I face her in school?" said Rory. "Jennifer will tell everyone that she saw me there."

Rory's mother, the optimist, shook her head. "I bet she won't. Never worry about something you're not sure of."

Rory bit her lip. She knew that wasn't such great advice. They weren't sure of how they'd pay the bills, and her mother worried about that all the time. She dug the toe of her tennis shoe into a crack in the linoleum.

And her mom just didn't realize what Jennifer might do. Her mother hadn't been there when Jennifer had told everyone to look at the label of her dress.

CHAPTER

Rory's mother was indeed wrong. First thing Monday morning, Jennifer said, "Rory, what were you doing with all those homeless people in the free food line?"

Thank goodness Ms. Bellini interrupted. "Jennifer, the bell has rung. Take your seat please," she said sternly.

Rory slunk down in her chair, never looking at Jennifer.

Chris turned around to draw on Rory's desk. Great. That's all she needed. Two creeps in the classroom.

To Rory, the day seemed two years long. It rained, so she couldn't even escape outside for recess. In the afternoon, she nearly fell asleep during the reading discussion.

She stared out the window at the drips falling from the drainpipe to the metal gutter below. Rain pelted the roof, drowning out Ms. Bellini's reading assignment.

Drip.

Oh no, thought Rory. *If it's raining, Mom will pick me up.*

Drip.

Everyone will see our old beat-up car.

Drip.

Rory stared out the window to the parking lot, searching for the old rusted car. She hoped her mother would come late. Then she drew in a sharp breath. Oh, no . . . there was her mother . . . pulling up right in front of the school!

"Rory?" Ms. Bellini's voice made Rory jump in her seat, and the class laughed. The bell rang, but Ms. B. continued.

"All right, class. We'll finish chapter three tomorrow."

Margie met Rory at the locker they shared.

"Boy, am I glad your mom is giving us a ride," said Margie as she pulled out her jacket.

"I'm not," said Rory.

"You mean you want to get soaked?" asked Margie.

"No, but if you had an old clunker of a car, you wouldn't want to be seen in it, either."

"Oh, Rory, it's no big deal," said Margie. "You're the only one who notices things like that."

Jennifer joined them as they walked out the school door.

"Wouldn't you know today is the day my mom's car is in the garage," said Jennifer, pushing her golden curls under the hood of her raincoat. "And it's really pouring, too."

"Over here!" waved Rory's mother as she stood under her bright orange umbrella. Rory saw her friends and classmates turn to stare at her mother. "Hi, girls!" Mrs. Mueller shouted.

"Hi, Mrs. Mueller," Margie called out.

Rory hunched over her books. *Oh, I just want to die,* she thought. Everyone in the whole school was there. They were all staring at her mother and their '64 Chevy.

Mrs. Mueller asked Jennifer, "Want a ride?"

Rory's mouth dropped open. How could her mother do that to her?

"Sure," said Jennifer.

Rory's mother climbed into the driver's seat. Jennifer tried to open the back door.

"I can't get it open," she said, struggling with the handle.

Rory frowned. "You have to jiggle it," she explained as she wiggled and pulled at it. Her wet hair dripped water down her back. She shivered and finally jerked the car door open. Jennifer and Margie slid in while Rory climbed into the front. A bouncing Charlie greeted her with a friendly lick.

Mrs. Mueller turned around and handed Jennifer her orange umbrella. She passed a green one to Margie. Margie opened it immediately.

"What are you doing?" asked Jennifer in a surprised voice.

Rory slumped down in her seat.

"You'll need it," said Rory's mother.

"It's a two-umbrella car," joked Margie.

They all fastened their seat belts as Rory's mother started the ignition and drove cautiously though the parking lot.

"Not much room back here," said Jennifer. She seemed irritated.

Rory turned and saw the girls eyeing the pails at their feet. Water dripped from the roof onto the umbrellas and ran down to the buckets on the floor. The open umbrellas bumped against each other. The buckets banged and clanged.

Plunk plunk plunk.

"Thanks for coming to get us, Mrs. Mueller," said Margie over the noise.

"No problem. I needed a break from my sewing. So how was school today?"

"Fine," said Rory, anxious to take everyone's mind off the old car. "Ms. Bellini said . . ."

Charlie crawled onto the front seat, appearing in front of Jennifer. He barked and wagged his tail. Water sprayed everywhere as he shook himself.

"Gross," mumbled Jennifer. "As if I'm not wet enough."

Then Charlie jumped onto her lap, placed his front paws on her shoulders, and licked her face noisily.

"Yuck!" she screamed. Jennifer covered her face with her hands. "Get this dripping dog off of me!"

Rory turned around, horrified. "Come here, Charlie!" She reached over the seat for the terrier. "Come on, sit with me."

In the commotion with Charlie, umbrellas had been forgotten, so now water dripped onto heads and noses. Margie smiled and grasped the green umbrella. Rory's mother chuckled. Charlie barked. But Rory just slumped further in her seat.

Margie poked her best friend. "Come on, Rory. It's funny! You don't see buckets and open umbrellas in cars every day."

By now, even Jennifer managed a grin.

"You're lucky, Rory," said Margie. "This car is better than my Aunt Jane's."

"I doubt it," grumbled Rory.

"Really. She has an old VW Bug with flowers painted on the outside. The backseat is missing, so she has pillows in there instead."

"You're kidding!" said Jennifer.

"But your car is better," added Margie.

Finally Mrs. Mueller pulled up to Jennifer's house.

"You need a new car," huffed Jennifer to Rory.

"This *is* our new car," said Rory.

CHAPTER

5

The bell rang and Rory stacked her books together.

"Hey, Margie, I'll walk home with you," shouted Jennifer over the after-school noise and confusion. Jennifer stood next to Margie, cutting her off from Rory.

"Sure," replied Margie.

Rory stared down at her shoes. So . . . her best friend was going to forget all about her and walk home with the new, popular girl.

Margie approached Rory. "Ready? Jennifer wants to walk home with us."

"*She's* going to come, too?" asked Jennifer, looking at Rory with raised eyebrows.

"Of course," said Margie. "We always walk

home together."

Rory stood closer to her ally. Jennifer looked Rory up and down. Rory was glad she had on a dress her mom had made, and not Jennifer's former dress. She'd taken that one and hidden it at the bottom of her closet. And she had made a vow never to wear it again.

"Let's go," said Margie. The three of them walked out of the school yard and down the block.

Jennifer picked a piece of lint from her designer jeans. "Did you see that gross shirt Barb had on today?"

Rory remembered that Barb sat behind Margie. But she couldn't remember the shirt Jennifer was talking about.

"It looked like something out of a thrift store!" Jennifer stared at Rory pointedly.

Rory fingered her worn jacket. Why did Jennifer have to butt in on her walk with Margie? Couldn't she hang out with someone else?

"Well, here we are," said Margie, jarring Rory back to reality. Margie reached into her purse to find her key.

Rory walked up her driveway. "See you tomorrow."

Margie dumped her bookbag on the sidewalk. "Hey, wait a minute. I can't find my key."

"Is it in one of your pockets?" asked Jennifer.

After a thorough search, Margie still couldn't find her key.

"Guess I must have left it on my dresser." She looked at Rory. "Can I come to your house until my mom comes home?"

"Sure," agreed Rory. "We can study for our history test."

"Say," said Jennifer. "I should study with you. Three heads are better than two."

"Good idea," said Margie.

Rory's eyes widened. What was Margie doing, inviting Jennifer to her house?

"Margie," said Rory. "Can I talk to you?"

Just then Mrs. Mueller appeared in the doorway. "The Lebkuchen is out of the oven. Anyone care for a snack?"

Margie and Jennifer ran to the front door. Rory followed, dragging her feet.

The girls sat down around the old green table, the one Rory's mother had found at a rummage sale.

"Oh, Mom, please don't buy it," Rory had begged. "It's so old-fashioned."

"Nonsense," her mother had replied. "It's a perfectly good table. We can buy it for practically nothing."

"Sure," said Rory. "Because nobody else wants it."

But her practical mother bought it—matching chairs and all.

Now Rory threw a dish towel over the empty chair to cover the rip in the seat. She picked up a spice cookie even though she didn't have much of an appetite.

"These cookies are great," said Margie, starting on her second.

"Lebkuchen is a German gingerbread cookie my mother taught me how to bake," said Mrs. Mueller.

"Mmm," said Margie.

"My mother gets French pastries from a bakery in the city," said Jennifer.

Just then, Rory's father came in the front door. He wore his old factory uniform with the paint splatters covering the front.

"Hi, Mr. Mueller," said Margie.

"Hi, girls," he greeted them cheerfully. He looked at Rory and then at Jennifer.

"Oh, Dad, this is Jennifer," said Rory reluctantly. Rory bet Jennifer's dad wore a suit and tie.

"Nice to meet you," Jennifer said politely.

Rory's dad kissed her mom on the cheek and grabbed some Lebkuchen. "I'm going to get cleaned up, and then I'll help you get rid of the rest of these cookies."

"Where do you work?" asked Jennifer, eyeing the paint stains.

"Down at the Furniture Factory," answered Mr. Mueller. "When I'm lucky, that is," he joked.

Rory slid further down on the plastic chair.

"See you later," he said as he walked down the hall.

Rory's mother filled their glasses with milk. "How was school?"

"Okay," said Rory, happy to get off the subject of her father's factory job. "But we're already having a history test. On Friday."

"And history is my worst subject," moaned Jennifer as she glanced around the room.

Rory followed Jennifer's eyes to the sewing table. Cut-out patterns and pieces of cloth lay everywhere. Broken thread and frayed material littered the floor.

Margie brushed crumbs off her hands. "Let's go into the living room to study."

Oh no, thought Rory. Everything in that room was *really* falling apart. She pulled Margie aside. "Margie," she whispered. "Don't take her in that room. Everything in there is old and worn out."

"Aw, come on, Rory. She won't care," said Margie as she joined Jennifer.

They filed into the living room. Rory tried to

steer them away from the couch. "Why don't we sprawl out on the floor?" she asked.

"This is fine," replied Jennifer as she sat down on the checkered sofa. The springs gave in. She sat down . . . down . . . down . . . rear end to the floor, feet high in the air.

"*UGH*! Get me out of here!" Jennifer's high-pitched screech could be heard throughout the house.

"Whoa! A people-eating couch!" giggled Margie.

Margie and Rory grabbed Jennifer's hands and pulled. Rory wanted to die. Why did Jennifer have to come over, anyway?

"Everything all right, girls?" asked Mrs. Mueller as she entered the room.

"That thing," Jennifer pointed to the beat-up couch, "gobbled me!" Jennifer, Margie, and Rory's mother roared with laughter.

"Shouldn't we get some work done?" asked Rory in an exasperated voice.

Her mother returned to her sewing, and the girls sat down on the faded rug. They spread their homework papers out before them.

"Do you think Ms. B. will ask any true-false questions?" asked Jennifer. "I hate true-false."

"Maybe it will be all multiple choice," suggested Margie hopefully.

The phone rang and Mrs. Mueller called out

from the kitchen. "Margie, your mother's on the phone. She says to come home right now."

Margie gathered her books together.

"I'd better go, too," said Jennifer. She glanced at the couch and smiled. "See you tomorrow, Rory. Does the rest of the class know about your hungry couch?"

Rory didn't answer. As soon as the girls left, she headed for her room.

"Are you okay, honey?" asked her mother as Rory passed the sewing machine.

"Just great," muttered Rory under her breath as her father came into the room.

"Rory," called her mother.

Rory slammed her bedroom door. She climbed onto her bed, next to Charlie. He opened one sleepy eye and wagged his tail. Rory buried her face in his fur. There was a knock on the door.

"Come in," said Rory, her voice muffled.

Rory's mother and father walked in and sat down on the bed. Rory felt a hand smooth her hair. For a moment, the only sound was Charlie's even breathing.

"What's wrong, Rory?" asked her dad.

"Everything." Rory spoke into the dog fur.

Her mother continued to smooth Rory's hair. "The couch?"

Rory lifted up her head. Tears welled in her eyes. "Oh, Mom, Dad," she cried. "It's the couch, our car, having to wear hand-me-downs and take handouts!" She spoke so quickly, all the words flowed together, like the tears falling on Charlie's fur. She gasped for breath.

"Being poor is so embarrassing. I can't stand for anyone to know about it. Especially someone rich and stuck-up like Jennifer. I wish I could hide forever!"

"Is she giving you a hard time?" asked her father as he reached for her hand.

"A hard time?" Rory pulled away from them and sat up straight. She wiped the tears from her face with the back of her hand.

"She reminds me all the time how rich she is. And anytime she can, she'll tell everybody how poor *I* am." Rory shuddered with the memory of her thrift-store dress. "Remember the blue dress we bought at Goodwill?"

Her mother nodded. "Yes. You liked it because of the color."

"Well, I don't like it anymore. It used to belong to Jennifer!"

"Oh, no," said her father.

Rory's mother sighed. "Honey, did Jennifer . . ."

"Yes," cried Rory. "In front of everyone."

"I'm so sorry, sweetie." Her mother hugged Rory. "You know it doesn't matter what things we have or don't have. Things don't make a person."

"I know. But they sure make Jennifer," said Rory bitterly, fingering the pattern on her bedspread.

"Well, then I feel sorry for her," said Rory's father. "She obviously doesn't have any confidence in her own personality to win people over."

"She's using me to make herself look good," said Rory, frowning.

Rory felt the tears begin again. "Tomorrow I'll have to hear her talk about our old couch."

"If she does, laugh with her," said Mr. Mueller. "If you make a joke of it, too, it won't be a big deal."

Laugh? Rory wondered if she'd ever laugh again.

CHAPTER

6

"Rory! Hurry up. You'll be late for school," called Mr. Mueller.

Rory grabbed her backpack. She hadn't realized how late it was. Now she'd have to ride her clunky old bike to school.

"Bye, Dad," she said as she ran out the back door. She threw off the burlap tarp that covered her bike and hopped onto the old-fashioned seat. Pedaling quickly, she noticed Margie riding ahead of her.

"Hey, Margie. Wait up!" Rory called.

But Margie didn't slow down. "Jennifer's up ahead," yelled Margie. "I'm going to catch up with her. See you at school."

Rory stopped racing and glided for a while. The crisp breeze blew her hair everywhere. Irritated, she brushed it away from her face, only for it to fly back again.

So Margie chose Jennifer instead of her. She felt a lump in her throat. Was she losing her best friend? As she rode the last block to school, she saw kids crowding into the building. The first bell must have rung.

Jumping off her bike, she looked around for a good hiding place. She wasn't going to park her ancient bicycle in the school rack ever again. The last time she did that, Chris had teased her for a week. No, she'd hide the old clunker from everyone. But where?

She tried stashing it behind Mrs. Johnson's evergreen, but the back tire stuck out in plain view. Rory studied the bush in the yard next door. She didn't know who lived there, but maybe no one would notice her bike if she pushed it way under the branches. She slid her bike into place and stood back to get a good view. Perfect. The bushes were large enough to hide the frame and tires, and thick enough so the metal didn't reflect in the sunlight.

Rory ran into the classroom just as the last bell rang. As she plopped into her seat, Chris sang under his breath, "Rory, Rory, Hallelujah."

Rory ignored him and watched Ms. B write the spelling words on the board.

"Eric," said Ms. B. "Could you put these words in alphabetical order?"

"Sure," said Eric as he walked up the aisle past Rory.

Rory studied him as he wrote on the chalkboard. Now why couldn't more boys be like Eric? He was nice to everyone. No wonder he was so popular. Eric finished and turned to face the class. There was just something about him. His blue eyes sparkled. A silver pendant hung around his shirt collar. Walking to his desk, he accidentally bumped against Rory. For a moment, their eyes met.

"Sorry," he whispered.

"It's okay," she said.

Eric flashed a smile that lit up his whole face. Rory felt a warm glow inside.

"Time for dictation," announced Ms. B.

Rory pulled out a piece of paper and wrote her name in the upper right-hand corner. Aurora Mueller . . . What if someday she and Eric . . . Rory wrote *Aurora Stevens* below her real name.

"Number one," said Ms. B.

Rory reached for her eraser, but the paper slid off the desk onto the floor. It landed beneath Barb's desk. Rory eyed it, trying to judge the distance between her and the paper. Even if she stretched every muscle, she'd never be able to reach it. What if someone saw it? She hadn't erased *Aurora Stevens*.

Barb moved her right foot, sliding the paper into the aisle. *Oh no,* thought Rory as she saw Chris glance at it. Turning around, he caught Rory's look. In the second their glances met, Chris grinned. Rory knew that grin. He knew she wanted that paper. She felt a blush starting at the base of her neck, creeping up her entire face.

Chris leaned way into the aisle, stretching his arm as far as he could. Rory held her breath, praying he wouldn't be able to grab it.

Fortunately it was just out of his grasp. He glanced at her just as she sighed with relief. He grinned again.

Uh-oh. What now? wondered Rory.

"Number two," said Ms. B.

Number two? What happened to number one? Rory had been so involved with her paper, she had missed the whole sentence. Quickly she grabbed another piece of paper.

"The neighbor rode his bicycle down the street," dictated Ms. Bellini.

Rory wrote the sentence and then looked up to see Chris slide down in his seat. Lower and lower he slid—until the top of his head was even with the top of his desk. He straightened his left leg until the toe of his tennis shoe rested on the paper. Rory bit her lip. Carefully Chris dragged his toe along the floor, dragging the paper with him. Rory felt her cheeks burn. She'd simply die when Chris read her name. And he'd probably read it aloud to everybody, too.

Suddenly the teacher walked over to them, bent down, and picked up the paper. Rory held her breath. Ms. B. glanced at it and then handed it to Rory. *Thank goodness Chris didn't get it,* she thought.

Ms. B. smiled slightly. Rory felt herself blush again.

As the recess bell rang, Rory opened her desk and quickly erased the evidence. Then she ran outside to meet Margie.

"Want to ride bikes to the park after school?" Jennifer asked Margie and Rory as they walked onto the playground.

"Sounds like fun," said Margie. "What about it, Rory?"

Rory shuffled her feet on the concrete. "Ah, no thanks."

"Why not?" asked Margie.

"I've got chores," fibbed Rory. She didn't want to give Jennifer a chance to comment about her old bike.

After school, Rory took a long time to gather up

her homework. She straightened her desk, then walked slowly down the hallway. Finally, when most of the kids had already left the building, she sauntered outside and over to the bush.

An elderly woman was standing on the front porch of the yard where Rory had hidden her bike. "Hello," she said.

"Hi," said Rory shyly. For a moment, neither of them spoke.

"Can I help you?" asked the woman.

Rory crossed into the yard. "My name is Rory Mueller, and I parked my bike behind your bush. I hope you don't mind."

The woman laughed. "No, not at all. Parking is free every weekday before five P.M."

Rory giggled as she pulled her bike onto the sidewalk.

"Say, is your mother Sarah Mueller?" asked the woman.

"Yes," said Rory.

"I'm Mrs. Mundsau. Your mother and I judged the Four H sewing contest together."

"Hey, Rory!" yelled a loud voice. "Sleeping Beauty!"

Oh, no. It was Creep-show Chris. She turned to see Chris, Eric, Margie, and Jennifer all headed her way.

CHAPTER

7

"Hi, Rory," said Margie.

"Hi," she tried to answer cheerfully as the girls pushed their bikes toward her. The boys carried skateboards.

"Where were you?" asked Jennifer.

"Oh, around," Rory answered vaguely, aware that Eric was staring at her bicycle.

"Can't get around too fast on that old clunker," teased Chris, his shaggy brown hair hanging over his eyes.

Rory looked down at the ground. Chris hit the wide metal bike frame with his hand. "Pretty ancient, huh? Did it come over on the *Mayflower*?"

Everybody laughed.

How could he be so mean? Rory pushed her

bike alongside Margie. Chris followed, with Jennifer and Eric bringing up the rear.

"Did you get problem sixteen in math?" Eric asked Jennifer.

As Rory continued to push her bike, she turned around to watch them.

"No. I'm not very good at math," said Jennifer as she slid her fingers through her hair. "Will you help me sometime?" She flashed him a smile.

Eric leaned closer to Jennifer and replied. But Rory couldn't hear what he said. At that moment, both Eric and Jennifer laughed, sharing a joke.

Rory fumed. What were they laughing about? She craned her neck to see them. Rory was so busy looking behind her that she didn't see the light pole in front of her.

"Augh!" she cried as she slammed into it.

"Rory, are you okay?" asked Margie.

"Sure," muttered Rory.

Chris burst out laughing. "Way to go, Rory! Did you hurt the light pole?"

Rory examined the front end of her bike. No dents, fortunately. Looking up, she caught Chris watching her. *Uh-oh. Here it comes again,* she thought.

"Why are you bothering to check your bike? You wouldn't be able to tell if you dented it or not!" Chris snickered.

Rory's cheeks burned. They reached her house and she turned into her driveway. Margie crossed the street to her home, while the others continued walking down the block.

"See you tomorrow, everyone," Margie called out. "Call me later, Rory."

Rory waved in response. The others called out their good-byes. *At least I'm home,* she thought. She hid her bike under the tarp and walked inside the house.

"Rory," called her father from the living room. "Come in here please. We need some help."

Rory found her mother and father at each end of the piano. "We've got to move this so we can clean behind it," explained her mother.

"Put your hands under the keyboard and help lift it," said Mr. Mueller.

After moving the piano, they found a surprise. There, where the piano had been a moment before, was a small pile of pills.

"What in the world!" exclaimed Mrs. Mueller.

Charlie darted past them and hid behind the couch.

"Charlie!" said Rory. "Those are *his* vitamins."

"Why, that little mutt," murmured her father.

Rory's mother put her hands on her hips. "That stinker. He's been eating the slices of cheese and spitting out the vitamin pills for weeks."

"But, Mom, he swallows every time."

"Charlie," called Rory's father. "Want a treat?"

Charlie came out from hiding, his tail wagging. They all headed for the kitchen.

"Here, Charlie," said Mrs. Mueller as she wrapped a slice of cheese around a pill. "Sit."

Charlie obeyed and Rory's mother held out the palm of her hand—the cheese in the middle. Charlie daintily picked it up, chewed for a moment, and then swallowed. Rory's mother gently pried open his jaws. The cheese had disappeared. But there, underneath his tongue, lay the pill.

Rory's mother placed the pill on the back of Charlie's tongue, closed his mouth, and held his jaws shut. With her left hand, she massaged his throat. Finally he gave in and swallowed. Rory's mother let go and Charlie bolted for the living room.

"There." Mrs. Mueller stood up. "We'll have to be more careful after this. We can't let that little terrier outsmart us."

Rory headed for the living room. She peered behind the piano where they had found the pills. There were none there now. Looking up, she saw Charlie dart out from behind the couch. Crossing the room, she peeked behind the sofa. There was a white pill.

"Mom! Dad!"

Mr. and Mrs. Mueller appeared, and Rory pointed behind the couch. Seeing the evidence, her mother gasped.

"Why, that clever little guy. Now what do we do?" Rory's father scratched his head. Charlie yawned and stretched out on the worn flowered rug.

"Guess we'll have to keep him in the kitchen after he swallows the pill," suggested Rory.

"Or else . . ." Her mother looked off into space. "I know." She walked quickly into the kitchen and opened the bottle of pills. Carelessly she dropped one onto the floor. "Oops. Oh, no. Rory, don't let Charlie get it," her mother cried as if it was a treasured morsel of food.

Rory bent down to retrieve the pill, but Charlie raced and gobbled it up. Licking his chops, he proudly marched to his dog bed and curled up for a nap.

"Good idea, hon," said Mr. Mueller.

"Pretty smart," complimented Rory. Her mom had just pretended not to care. Then Rory had an idea. Maybe that's what *she* should do with Chris. If she didn't let him know he bugged her, perhaps he'd stop being so annoying. After all, he did seem to like it when she got mad. Rory reached down to pet Charlie. Would that work with Jennifer, too?

CHAPTER

8

Rory fastened Charlie's leash and he pulled her down the sidewalk.

"You ready?" yelled Margie from across the street.

"Yeah! Charlie's been waiting for his walk all afternoon."

Margie crossed the street, hands in her jeans pockets. "I wish my mom would let me get a dog," she muttered.

Charlie wagged his tail in greeting. Just as they began their neighborhood walk, a large black Lab bounded from a side street.

"Oh, no," worried Rory aloud. "I hope Charlie doesn't see—"

But it was too late. He did. With one quick pull

on the leash, Rory jerked forward. She tried to plant her feet firmly on the ground, but Charlie surged ahead. The leash flew from Rory's hand. Charlie, now free, ran after the Lab. The large dog, catching sight of the terrier, froze for a moment and then bolted down the sidewalk, Charlie in hot pursuit.

Rory and Margie both screamed at once. "Charlie! Stay!"

But Charlie didn't listen. His little legs followed the long strides of the big dog. *"Ruff, ruff!"* he yipped.

"Arr arr!" yelped the Lab, galloping away as if in pain.

Rory chased after Charlie. "Come back here!"

"Here's a treat, Charlie," said Margie as she tried to bribe the terrier.

It didn't work.

Suddenly Rory gasped. The intersection of Main and Madison was dead ahead. The center of town—with cars everywhere.

Breathless, Rory ran as fast as she could. She had to stop those dogs. She knew Charlie would never pay attention to cars while he was in a chase.

She became aware of another runner joining in the chase. Glancing to her side, she saw Eric. Why was he running with them?

The black Lab turned abruptly before the crosswalk and ran through a neatly kept yard. Trampling through the flower beds, a vegetable garden, and a children's play yard, Charlie finally cornered the huge dog.

The Lab whined and backed up against a fence. Charlie put on his brakes and skidded to a halt, nearly bumping into the dog that was five times his size.

Margie reached them first. But before she could bend down to grab the terrier, Charlie looked up at the Lab, barked once, shook himself, and trotted calmly to Rory.

"What in the world?" said Margie.

"Guess he just wanted to show us who's boss," laughed Rory.

"Come on, Cocoa," called Eric.

"Cocoa?" asked Rory. "Is that your dog?"

"Yes," said Eric sheepishly. "She's afraid of everything."

"I'm so s-s-sorry," stammered Rory. "Charlie is always chasing animals bigger than he is."

"Guess he has to prove something because he's so small." Eric grabbed Cocoa's collar and attached her leash. "Sorry she got away from me," he apologized. "Cocoa started out chasing a squirrel."

"Until Charlie started chasing her," Margie giggled. "It's kind of funny, you know."

Rory set Charlie down and wrapped the leash securely around her left hand. With her right, she tucked her blouse into her jeans and tried to smooth her windblown hair. She was a mess. Turning away from Eric, she pretended to adjust Charlie's leash while she wiped the beads of perspiration off of her forehead. Every hair on Eric's head lay in place. *How could he look so perfect?* wondered Rory as she faced him with a hesitant smile.

"Maybe we should leave this yard before someone gets mad at us," said Eric, pulling Cocoa after him as he headed toward the sidewalk.

Margie and Rory followed, with Charlie trotting behind Cocoa as though nothing had happened.

Rory searched her mind for something to say to Eric. Should she toss back her hair like Jennifer had done? Should she ask him if he liked baseball?

"Er . . . ah . . ." she stumbled over her words. "Doyoulikebaseball?"

Eric turned to her, a puzzled expression on his face. "What?"

The words flew out of Rory's mouth again. "Doyoulikebaseball?"

"Yeah. It's okay," answered Eric.

There was an awkward silence. Talking to Eric was a lot harder than she expected. What should she say now? Rory looked at Margie for help. Margie gestured to Eric's dog. Rory frowned, but then she caught on.

"How old is Cocoa?" she asked.

"She'll be four in December."

"Really? Charlie will be four in December, too." Rory smiled in surprise. *Why, they could have a double birthday party,* she thought. Rory pictured party hats on all of the neighborhood canines.

"What's so funny?" asked Eric.

"Well . . ." began Rory, hesitant to admit her silly idea.

"Go on, Rory," said Eric encouragingly.

"Well, since both dogs are going to be four, they could have a double birthday party together."

"A dog party? What fun!" said Margie.

"Dog biscuits could be the party favors," said Eric.

"With pin-the-tail-on-the-cat as the party game!" added Margie.

Rory forgot to be self-conscious. "Instead of birthday cake, they could have birthday bones!"

Eric stopped walking and faced the girls. "Hey, you know we could really do it."

"Wouldn't it be fun?" asked Margie.

"We could invite all the dogs in the class," said Rory, excited.

"You mean all the kids' dogs," corrected Eric, grinning.

"Yes, that's what I meant," Rory laughed, not even embarrassed at her mistake. Just think, planning a party with Eric. *This is great!* she thought happily.

Margie whipped out a notebook from her back pocket. "I'll make a list of all the things we need to do," she said.

They reached the corner where Charlie had started chasing Cocoa.

"See you tomorrow. Let's keep this idea a secret, okay?" said Eric.

"Fine," replied Rory. Wow. Sharing a secret with Eric. Dreamily she watched him walk down the street.

CHAPTER

9

The next day, Rory couldn't wait for school to begin. She spent extra time in the bathroom, experimenting with new hairstyles. She was tired of her straight blond hair.

Pulling it away from her face, Rory bunched the ends into a ball on top of her head. *Hmm. Different.* It certainly made her look more grown-up, but she knew that after five minutes, the small hairs would fall out of the bun and stick out of her head like porcupine spikes. No, that certainly wouldn't do.

She let her hair drop to her shoulders. Tilting her head to the side, she tossed back her hair the way Jennifer had done and tried to imagine her face framed in soft curls.

Then Rory had an idea. Quickly brushing her hair until it shined, she ran out of the bathroom to the kitchen, where her mother had already begun the day's sewing.

"Hey, Mom, can I get a perm?" She held her breath, waiting for the answer. The right answer.

Mrs. Mueller took the pins out of her mouth and smiled. "Why, Rory, I didn't think you cared about your hair."

Rory cleared her throat. "I don't. I'm just sick of my long hair."

"You know, Rory, permanents are expensive. Althea's Beauty Salon charges fifty dollars."

Rory pulled out the kitchen chair and sat down. Picking up her spoon, she stirred her cereal. Fifty dollars? Why, even if she mowed lawns and washed cars for a month she'd never earn that kind of money.

"But there's always a home permanent," added her mother as she fitted a dress on a dummy.

"A home permanent?"

"Yes. We can buy one for a few dollars at the drugstore, and I can apply it right here, at home."

Rory jumped up. "Oh, Mom, would you? Could you?"

"Sure. I did your Aunt Ann's hair all through high school. Everyone thought she had natural curls."

"Oh, thanks, Mom!" Rory threw her arms around her mother.

"Why don't you take some of your lawnmowing money and go to the drugstore after school? I can give you a perm tonight after supper."

"Great!" Rory ran to her room for the money and grabbed her books. Hugging Charlie, she paused so he could give her a wet lick on her nose before they bounded downstairs.

"Bye, Mom," she yelled as she opened the screen door.

Charlie barked.

"But Rory, your breakfast . . ."

"No time today. See you after school." With that Rory ran to tell Margie the news.

"So your mom said yes?" asked Margie.

Rory nodded, thinking of the soft curls that would gently bounce on her shoulders after tonight. She couldn't wait.

"Don't tell anyone, okay, Margie? I want it to be a surprise."

"All right." Margie kicked the maple leaves at her feet as they walked to school. "I wonder what Eric will say?"

Rory caught her breath and looked at Margie suspiciously. "What do you mean?"

"Well, the way you stuttered and stammered yesterday about baseball, it was pretty obvious."

"Oh, no!" Rory groaned. "Do you think he knows I like him?" She zipped her jacket against the November wind.

"Don't worry," said Margie. "Boys don't always pick up on things like that."

"Has Jennifer talked about Eric at all?" Rory bit her lip. Even with curls, Rory knew she would be no match for cute and bubbly Jennifer.

"No. She just flirts a lot."

"She's so fake," grumbled Rory.

"Oh, Jennifer's all right. She just likes to show off sometimes."

"Sometimes. *Ha!* She shows off all the time in front of Eric."

Rory opened the door to the school building. The heat from the furnace hit her face. The first bell rang just as they closed their locker door.

Rory hurried to the classroom and slid into her seat.

"How's Charlie?" Eric asked as he opened his math book.

"Fine. And Cocoa?"

"She's okay." Eric rolled his eyes. "A cat chased her down the block just before school."

Rory laughed until Jennifer tapped Eric on the

shoulder. "Eric, do you have the math assignment?"

Eric shuffled some papers and read off the page numbers.

Ooh, that Jennifer, Rory thought. *Just when I get a chance to talk to him,* she *ruins it.*

"Good morning, class," said Ms. B. "Today before the announcements, I'd like you to sign up for a 'country' report in social studies. Write your name and choice of nation on a piece of paper, and pass it forward."

Rory smiled, tore off a sheet of paper and wrote "Germany" along with her name. Great! She knew a lot about Germany. This was going to be fun. Rory handed the paper to Barb and worked at the five daily math problems on the board.

"I have tabulated all of the countries and now have your assignments," said Ms. B. "Jennifer, Craig, Alison, and Eric will report on Ireland."

Rory's heart sank as she saw Jennifer and Eric smile at each other. They were assigned to the same country.

Ms. B. continued, "Margie, Rick, and Susan will research China."

Rory saw Margie smile. Lucky Margie. She already knew a lot about China from her parents.

"Chris, Rory, Barb, and Jeff will study Germany."

Ms. B. continued with her lists, but Rory stopped paying attention. Not only were Jennifer and Eric paired together, but Rory had Chris in her group.

ZING!

Rory felt something hit her forehead. She looked down at the floor. A wet, gray spitball lay beneath her chair. Chris stuck out his tongue at her. Remembering her new pledge not to be annoyed by him, Rory turned right back to her work as though nothing had happened.

She almost smiled when she noticed that Chris looked glum. Her plan might work after all. And tonight she'd get a new look to go along with her new personality. She could hardly wait.

CHAPTER 10

That night, Rory read the home-permanent solution box as she sat waiting for the timer.

"Cover rods with plastic cap. Test curl every five minutes."

Pinching her nose, she glanced up to see her mother laughing.

"It does have an awful odor," Mrs. Mueller agreed.

"It stinks!" she cried.

"What price beauty?" commented her mother.

Charlie barked and wagged his tail as Rory's dad came in through the screen door.

"Pieeuie!" He pretended to be horrified when he saw his daughter. Shielding his face with his arms, he screamed, *"EECH!* A Martian."

"Oh, Dad." Rory rolled her eyes. She loved to greet her father when he came home from work. He always smelled of freshly sawed wood. But now the odor of the perm was so strong, it made her eyes water and her nose burn. She couldn't smell anything except her own hair.

"*BZZ.*" Rory reached across the table to turn off the timer. Her mother unrolled a curler to test her hair.

"Why, I do believe it's done."

"Done?" asked her father, choosing an apple from the fruit bowl. "As in baked?"

Rory smiled. The phone rang and Mrs. Mueller answered it.

"The treasury report is due tomorrow night?" she asked. Rory's mother was the treasurer of the town's historical society.

"Does Marilyn have the receipts for the German fair?"

German fair. That reminded her of the social-studies project. Germany. She had a great idea. She had better write it down before she forgot. Jumping up, Rory ran to her bedroom.

"What did I do with that notebook," she muttered, rummaging though her desk drawers. "Ah-ha." She grabbed the spiral binder and opened to a blank page. "Germany report," she wrote. "Lebkuchen, Bach."

"Rory," her mother called from the kitchen. "Let's get those curlers out."

"Okay, Mom," she said as she raced down the stairs, her wet hair dripping on the towel draped around her shoulders.

The doorbell rang.

"That's probably Margie. I'll get it," she yelled. She threw the front door open and came face to face with Eric.

She gasped as her hands flew automatically to her head.

Eric's eyes widened. For a moment neither of them said anything. Rory felt water dripping down her back.

"I'm looking for Rory," said Eric as a huge grin appeared on his face.

"I—I—" Rory stuttered.

"Oh, it's you. Get caught in a rainstorm?"

Rory couldn't speak.

"Well, hello there," boomed her father from the hallway. He extended his hand to Eric. "I'm Mr. Mueller."

"Hi. I'm Eric Stevens."

"Come in," said Mr. Mueller. "If you can stand the smell."

Rory wished she were invisible.

"Don't mind Rory," continued her father. "She might be a big drip today, but tomorrow she's going to be gorgeous."

"Oh, Dad," mumbled Rory, staring at the puddle beneath her.

Mrs. Mueller walked into the entryway. "Hi, Eric. I just talked to your mother on the phone. How nice of you to pay us a visit."

Eric turned to Rory. "I came over to see if you still wanted to have a dog party," he said.

"A dog party?" asked Rory's mother.

"My Lab, Cocoa, and Charlie both have birthdays in December."

"So we thought we'd have a party for them," finished Rory, wiping drips of water off of her forehead with the towel.

"That's a wonderful idea," said Mrs. Mueller.

"Do you want to use our backyard?" asked Mr. Mueller.

"Hey, that would be great," Eric nodded.

"When should we have it?" asked Rory, almost forgetting how she looked.

Rory's mom studied the calendar hanging on the wall. "How about the first weekend in December?"

"That's perfect," said Rory. "Then we'll have time to make the invitations."

After Eric left, Rory closed the door and leaned her wet head against it.

"Oh, Mom," she groaned. "He saw me in curlers!"

Her mother shrieked. "Curlers! I forgot! Rory, we've got to take those out right now."

CHAPTER
11

Rory sat, head bent backward over the sink. "Oh Mom," she cried. "He saw me in curlers. I looked awful." Tears welled in her eyes.

"I'm sorry for you Rory, but you know, the first time your father and I went out on a date, a plate of spaghetti landed in my lap."

"Really? How did that happen?"

Her mother took out the last curler and ran warm water through her hair. "We had gone out to a fancy Italian restaurant and I ordered spaghetti. When the waiter came with the food, I was so busy flirting with your father that I forgot to take the napkin off the placemat. Then the waiter put the plate on top of the napkin. When I pulled the edge of the napkin, the plate flipped over into my lap."

"What did you do then?"

Her father came into the kitchen and planted a wet kiss on Rory's forehead. "She put the spaghetti back on the plate and ordered lasagna instead."

Finally Mrs. Mueller wrapped a towel around Rory's head.

"Why don't I try the blow-dryer, and then we'll experiment with my curling iron," she suggested.

"Sure, Mom."

Rory sat down on a kitchen chair while her mother returned from the bathroom with the blow dryer. Mrs. Mueller carefully pulled her hair outward with a brush and then flipped it up. Rory started to feel better as the heat warmed her head and neck. Soon she'd be beautiful.

"Oh, my. Oh, my," said her mother.

"Oh, my, what?" asked Rory.

"Oh, my," said her father.

"Ruff!" Charlie barked as he ran and hid under the table.

"Oh, my," repeated her mother.

Slowly Rory picked up a hand mirror. Her hair was a giant mass of frizz. What would everyone say at school? She looked awful. Rory let out a sob and ran out of the kitchen.

Once in the bathroom, she gazed into the mirror through her tears. Everywhere, hair tightly coiled like springs stuck out six inches from her head. She couldn't believe how bad it was.

Why, she looked even worse than when Eric had caught her in curlers. Even worse than the time she chewed gum and blew a huge bubble that popped all over her face and hair. Her mother worked for two hours to get it out before she finally cut it off, leaving short blotchy patches all over her head.

But she looked worse now. Rory felt tears spill onto her cheeks, and she sat down on the rim of the bathtub, head in her hands. Charlie whined beside her.

"Rory? Are you all right?" called her mother from downstairs.

"Yes, Mom." Rory quietly stifled another sob.

Mom would feel awful if she knew she was so upset, but what was she going to do? She turned on the blow-dryer to muffle her cries and laid it on the countertop.

Laying her head in her arms, she cried and cried. She sobbed for her ugly hair, for Chris's mean remarks that were sure to follow, and for Jennifer's snobbishness. She cried until a wet black nose pushed its way between her arms to find her face. Charlie's pink tongue lapped up the tears and she lifted her head. He jumped in her lap.

"Oh, Charlie," Rory whispered, hugging him tight. "You love me no matter what I look like, don't you?"

"Rory," her mother called again.

Quickly she tore off some toilet paper, wiped her nose, and set Charlie down. She picked up the dryer and grabbed a brush.

"I'm up here," she answered, staring at herself in the mirror. "Maybe I can style it," she thought aloud. "Like they do on TV."

She turned the brush under her hair, winding the twisted frizz around it. Then she lifted it up and pulled. And pulled. Then she yanked. It wouldn't budge. Her brush was stuck in the newly permed frizz. New tears appeared as she continued trying to free it. But that only made it worse. Charlie pawed her leg.

"Oh, Charlie," sniffed Rory, bending down to the terrier, the heavy brush dangling from her head. "What am I going to do?"

CHAPTER

12

"Hey, Aurora, who chopped off your hair?" teased Chris as he strolled into the classroom before school began.

Rory ignored Chris's remark and opened her social-studies notebook.

"Isn't it cool? It's what all the New York models are wearing," Margie said, jumping to Rory's defense.

"What a neat haircut," said Barb. "It makes you look thirteen."

"Did you have it done in the city?" asked Jennifer. "I have mine done at Chez Elegance. My mom says Althea's is old-fashioned."

"No, I didn't get it cut in the city," said Rory, trying not to laugh. What would Jennifer say if she knew that her mother cut it to free a brush from a pile of frizz?

"Her mother styled it," said Margie. "Isn't she good? I wish my mom could cut my hair."

Jennifer tossed her curls. "My mother's too busy with her court cases to bother to cut my hair."

"Too bad," said Chris, doodling on his desk. "You need all the help you can get."

Ms. B. cleared her throat. "Today we'll begin by meeting in our social-studies groups to work on the reports. They're due on Friday."

Rory glanced at Eric. He smiled. She smiled back, then lowered her gaze as she touched her hair, winding a short curl around her finger. *What a wonderful feeling,* she thought. A brand-new look . . . a brand-new Rory.

After school, as Rory pulled her bike out from behind the bushes, she heard someone say her name. Turning around, she saw Mrs. Mundsau on the front porch of her house.

"Hi," said Rory, wheeling her bike onto the sidewalk.

"Would you like to come in for some cookies?" asked Mrs. Mundsau.

Rory smiled. Cookies sounded great. She parked

her bike behind the bushes again and bounded up the porch steps.

The screen door squeaked as Rory followed Mrs. Mundsau into the house. Once inside, Rory came face-to-face with an old photograph of a bride and groom. They looked very young. The bride's hair was piled on top of her head. Ringlet curls hung in front of her ears. The bride's lacy dress draped to the floor.

"I was twenty when I got married, and Harry was twenty-one."

"You were beautiful," said Rory. "And he was handsome."

Mrs. Mundsau smiled. "Harry was quite a charmer. There was a full moon the night he asked me to marry him. We danced under the stars. We danced without music!" Then she sighed and her face became grim. "It was before the war. The terrible war."

"Did your husband have to fight in it?" asked Rory.

Mrs. Mundsau shook her head. "No, thank goodness. He had a back problem, so they didn't make him." She touched the frame delicately. "The war years were difficult for everyone. My best friend . . ." Her voice trailed off.

Rory guessed the truth. "She died?"

"Yes. The soldiers came before she had a chance to hide." She led Rory into the living room. "We had it all planned. She was to hide in our basement."

Rory sat down on an old-fashioned chair. "When did you come here?"

"We left when the war ended. There were too many sad memories there. And we wanted to live in a democracy—where everyone would be equal."

Rory sat back in her chair and looked around. It was a cozy little room. Lace doilies covered chairs and the coffee table in front of them. An intricate pattern of vines was carved into the table's legs. Rory gently touched the pattern of flowers on the table's edge. "Art in a table!"

Mrs. Mundsau handed Rory a cup of tea. "It's very old. We had it shipped from Germany." Then Mrs. Mundsau laughed. "Of course everything in this house is old. Just like me!" She set her cup down. "I've lived here fifty years, and I haven't changed any of the furniture." She smiled. "I like it all because it reminds me of Harry. He died five years ago."

"I'm sorry," said Rory.

"Don't be, dear." She picked up a cookie. "We had a wonderful life together."

Rory looked around the room. Why did old look good here, but not in her house? She noticed there was a chip in the teacup she held. She rubbed the rough spot with her finger. If her mother had this cup, Rory would have hated it. But somehow it felt comforting here.

"The china set belonged to my grandmother," said Mrs. Mundsau. "I don't have many pieces of the set left."

Rory bit into some Lebkuchen. Suddenly, she had an idea. A great idea. A simply wonderful idea. "Mrs. Mundsau, would you do me a great big favor?"

CHAPTER

13

The week passed quickly, with Rory's German report occupying all of her free time. On Friday Ms. Bellini said Rory's group could present their report right after morning recess.

"Great," said Chris. "Then we can set everything up during the break."

"Good idea," said Rory. For once she agreed with Chris. In fact, during the past few days, he never turned around to annoy her. If he turned around at all, it was to show her the map of Germany he was working on.

When the rest of the class filed out to the playground, Rory's group stayed behind. Rory and Chris hung posters around the room, and Barb and Jeff passed out plates and napkins.

"It's a good thing we're doing this in the morning before lunch," said Barb. "So we'll all be starving."

The night before, the kids had been at Rory's house making all of the food. Mrs. Mundsau had shown them how to make strudel, Rory's dad helped with the sauerbraten, and Rory taught everyone how to make Lebkuchen.

Rory tore off a piece of masking tape and made a tape roll. As she pasted it to the back of a poster, she glanced up to see Chris staring at her. He blushed when she caught him, and he hurriedly pounded a poster onto the chalkboard with his fist. *Hmm.* Maybe he didn't really hate her after all.

They finished decorating the room just as the bell rang.

Rory began the report by talking about Germany's geography. Chris and Barb discussed history, and Jeff told everyone about the food they would serve. When they passed out the treats, the class *mmmm*ed and *yummm*ed.

"The strudel is great," said Margie as she licked her fingers. "You guys should get an A."

When Mrs. Mundsau walked into the room, Rory put down the tray of cookies and went to the front of the class to introduce her. "I'd like for you all to meet a friend of mine. This is Mrs. Mundsau. She lived in Germany for twenty-five years."

Mrs. Mundsau talked about her life in Germany and when she and her husband came to America. "We weren't rich," she said. "But that didn't matter."

Rory followed Mrs. Mundsau's gaze straight to Jennifer. Jennifer looked down at her painted fingernails.

Mrs. Mundsau continued. "In America it doesn't matter what religion you believe in or how much money you have. You're all equal."

Ha, thought Rory. *That shows Jennifer.* She caught Mrs. Mundsau's glance and smiled. Mrs. Mundsau knowingly smiled back.

And then something dawned on Rory. Maybe that message wasn't really meant for Jennifer after all.

CHAPTER 14

COME TO A PARTY
HAPPY BIRTHDAY CHARLIE AND COCOA
WHERE—1212 LOCUST STREET
WHEN—SATURDAY, DECEMBER 2ND, 2–4 PM

Eric and Rory spread a large picnic tablecloth on the floor of the basement. Eric surveyed the space.

"It's too bad it's snowing or we could have had this in your backyard."

"It will still be fun," said Rory, running upstairs to answer the doorbell.

"Your mom is really nice to let us have the party in here," Eric called after her.

Rory ran to the front door, Charlie and Cocoa barking at her heels.

"Hi," said Margie, taking off her snow boots. "Sorry I don't have a puppy to bring. But here's a present for the birthday dogs." She handed over a package wrapped in poodle-covered paper. "This is going to be fun!"

Rory hoped so. But since Margie had insisted on inviting Jennifer, she wasn't so sure.

"Come downstairs," she said. "Eric's already here."

In the basement, Charlie and Cocoa sniffed at the present and started to whine. Rory put the gift on top of the washing machine. "Oh, no, you two. You have to wait until your other guests get here to unwrap your presents."

As Eric placed six paper plates on the tablecloth, Cocoa playfully scampered onto the covering and rolled over, scratching her back.

"Now cut that out, Cocoa," yelled Eric, pushing the big Lab away and straightening the paper plates. Each plate had a large bone drawn on it, marked with the name of a dog.

The doorbell rang again. Eric glanced at his watch. "It's two o'clock. They're here."

The guests and their dogs clumped noisily down the wooden stairs. Jennifer led the group. She smiled in her designer overalls. Rory looked down at her worn jeans. Mrs. Mueller followed with her camera.

"Esther, Esther!" called Barb to her Saint Bernard. Esther's leash was tangled with Jeff's cocker spaniel.

"*Ruff, ruff,*" barked the spaniel.

Esther just looked at him.

"Hold on, Snickers," Jeff said to his dog as he tried to get the two canines free from each other.

Jennifer's poodle, Muffy, yipped at Chris's German shepherd, Tiny. Cocoa explored the boxes stacked near the washing machine.

CRASH! Kids and dogs ran to examine the scattered boxes.

"Hope there weren't any dishes in there," said Eric, grabbing Cocoa's collar and trying to drag her away from the mess.

Mrs. Mueller laughed. "No, just material for the dresses I make. Don't worry about it."

Eric turned to Rory. "Boy, you sure do have a great mom," he said.

"I do?" she said as she watched her mom snap a few pictures of the chaos.

"Yes," he said.

Rory smiled. "I guess I do."

Jennifer tapped Eric on the shoulder. "Oh Eric," she purred. "Will you please help me? Muffy won't come when I call her. Can you catch her for me?"

"Sure," said Eric, handing Cocoa over to Rory. "Here, Rory, hold her, will you?" He chased after Muffy.

"Here she is," he said, handing the poodle to Jennifer.

"Oh, thank you," Jennifer gushed.

Rory couldn't stand it a minute longer. She clapped her hands. "Okay, everybody. Get your dogs to sit in a line for the relay races."

Jennifer stood close to Eric, setting Muffy down next to Cocoa. Cocoa whined.

Chris bent to pet Cocoa on the head. "What's the matter ol' girl? Can't stand Miss Muffy's perfume, can you? It sure does stink."

Everyone laughed. The smell of expensive perfume circled Muffy and Jennifer like a cloud.

"It's better than smelling like a dog," sniffed Jennifer.

"Well, you should know!" howled Chris.

Margie looked at the list on her clipboard. "Hey, Rory. Let's start the races."

"Good idea," said Mrs. Mueller. She sat on the dryer, away from the confusion.

Rory stood in the line of wriggling dogs. The owners all held their dogs by their collars as they watched Eric lay a row of dog biscuits on the finish line. Rory had two dogs to control: Charlie and Cocoa.

"Get ready . . . get set . . ." began Eric.

"Hey, wait a minute," said Jennifer. "Let Muffy have a head start."

"Why?" asked Margie, the judge of the race.

"Because it's not fair," Jennifer whined. "My poodle is no match for a German shepherd."

"But small dogs run fast," said Margie. Jennifer frowned and Eric continued.

"Get ready . . . get set . . . go!" he yelled.

The canines rushed to the treats, but not in straight relay lines. Crisscrossing in all directions, the yelping dogs bumped and barked their way to the finish.

The slobbering Saint Bernard swallowed his dog biscuit and lapped up another. Jennifer began to protest as she watched the hulking hound eat Muffy's treat.

"Better give Muffy a bone," suggested Rory.

"Okay," said Eric, reaching for the box of treats.

The sound of the box opening brought all the dogs running for more. They clamored in front of Eric, jumping and bouncing around him.

"Hey, you guys, get down," Eric ordered, lifting the box high above his head. "Esther, get down this minute," said Barb, trying to move Esther's paws off Eric's shoulders.

Esther pounced on Eric—all two hundred pounds of her.

"*Woof,*" she said as she lapped his face with a large wet tongue.

"Yuck." Eric made a face as he fell backward. The box flew out of his hands. Dog bones flew everywhere.

A flash of light blinded Rory as she reached out for Charlie's collar. She looked up to see her mother in hysterics, taking pictures as fast as she could.

"Snickers, get over here," demanded Jeff.

"Tiny . . . *SIT*," said Chris. The huge dog sat. Right on Muffy.

"*Yelp!*" cried Muffy.

Tiny jumped up. "*Ruff.*"

"My poor baby," said Jennifer, cradling the poodle. Muffy wriggled free and joined her friends in finding dog biscuits.

Crunch crunch crunch.

"Sorry, Mom," Rory shouted over the din of crunching, barking, and yelling.

Her mother lowered her camera and laughed. "Not exactly your usual birthday party," she shouted across the room.

Finally, when the dog biscuits disappeared, the dogs quieted down enough for Mrs. Mueller to announce, "Cake time!"

The dogs gathered around for their treats of rawhide bones. Rory's mother passed out chocolate cake to their owners.

Jennifer sat across from Rory and Eric at the table.

"Hey, Rory," Eric leaned closer to her. "Isn't this a great party?"

"Say, Eric," Jennifer interrupted. "Have you tried Rory's old couch?"

"What?" asked Eric, puzzled.

"More cake anyone?" offered Rory.

"Rory has a man-eating couch," continued Jennifer.

"Great," Chris said. "You should sit in it."

Everyone laughed. Everyone but Jennifer, whose eyes blazed angrily.

She turned to Rory. "My father is a doctor," she continued.

"We know," said Chris, pretending to snore. "You've only told us that about a hundred times. Real exciting."

Jennifer stared down at her plate.

"Boy, we're so glad you never brag," Chris went on. "Don't you ever get tired of talking about yourself?"

For once, she was speechless. The room was quiet. Rory thought Jennifer was going to cry.

"Hey, Jennifer," Rory said slowly. "You should have seen what happened to me the other day."

"What happened?" asked Barb.

"Well, a perm sort of fried my hair," said Rory.

"Is that why you cut your hair?" asked Jennifer.

Rory nodded. "Yes."

"Hey, we forgot to sing 'Happy Birthday'," said Margie, examining her notebook.

"Let's do it now," said Eric, licking the last of the frosting from his fork.

Rory turned off the lights and Mrs. Mueller lit eight candles on the cake as everyone joined in singing. Both Cocoa and Charlie were four years old. The dogs, as if on cue, barked in unison.

"How are Charlie and Cocoa going to blow out their candles?" asked Barb.

"Eric and Rory should blow them out," suggested Margie.

The second before Rory blew, she looked up and met Eric's gaze. She made a wish—then there was darkness.

"Yeah!" Everyone clapped and cheered. Mrs. Mueller flipped the light switch.

While the dogs chewed their bones, Eric set a tub of water on the plastic tablecloth. Soon the six dogs were nosing their way to the water dish.

Lap lap lap.

"They sure are noisy," said Jeff.

Mrs. Mueller looked out of the basement window. "It's stopped snowing. Anyone for a snowball fight before the party's over?"

Kids and dogs flew up the stairs.

"Wait. We should clean up," suggested Margie.

Mrs. Mueller waved her hand. "Don't worry about it. We'll do it later."

"Good-bye, Mrs. Mueller," said Barb. "Thank you."

Good-byes and thank-yous echoed up the stairs and out the front door.

Rory felt a snowball hit her back. Turning, she saw Chris duck behind a bush. She packed snow into a ball and hid it in her coat pocket. Throwing a stick to Cocoa for a game of fetch, she pretended to focus all of her attention on the dogs, while watching Chris out of the corner of her eye.

She saw him sneak out from behind the bush. *Smack!* The snowball hit him right on his behind as he turned his back to her. Chris whipped around and smiled. Moments later, snowballs were flying everywhere.

"Yippeeee!" screamed Margie.

"Having fun?" asked Rory, ducking from a whizzing snowball.

"This is the best party ever," said Margie.

Jennifer attached Muffy's leash to her collar. "Thanks for inviting us."

Charlie lay down next to Muffy in the snow and whined.

"I don't think he wants Muffy to leave," said Rory.

Muffy nuzzled Charlie's fur with her nose.

"They're in love," cried Jennifer.

"Well, Jennifer, you'll have to come over again and bring Muffy," said Rory, surprised at her own invitation.

"Can I?" Jennifer blurted. She blushed.

"Sure. The dogs will have a lot of fun together," said Rory. "And maybe we can, too."

CHAPTER
15

The doorbell rang and Rory pulled on her snow jacket.

"Hi," said Eric as she opened the door. Falling snowflakes drifted in. "It's really snowing out here."

"All right!" Rory clapped her mittened hands together. "Maybe we'll have a snow day."

"No chance," called Mrs. Mueller from the kitchen. "I've been listening to the radio and your school didn't close."

"Maybe they'll let us go home at noon," Eric replied, brushing the snow off of his boots before coming into the hallway.

Mrs. Mueller appeared, putting a cap over her head. "I'll give you kids a ride today. I've got the car."

"Thanks," said Eric. "Now we won't get wet."

Rory smiled. "Don't bet on it."

Rory and Eric helped Mrs. Mueller take the bricks and old blankets off the car.

"Boy, I wish we had a garage," said Mrs. Mueller.

"No, you don't," said Eric. "Then you'd have to clean it. Ours is full of junk all the time."

Rory removed the last piece of cardboard covering the windshield. "Every night it takes us twenty minutes to put this car to bed. It has more quilts and blankets than we do."

Rory's mother inserted her key into the door.

"That's funny," she said, wiggling the handle.

"What's the matter?" asked Eric.

"The door won't open. The lock must have frozen shut."

"Try the passenger door," suggested Rory.

Mrs. Mueller walked around to the other side of the car. The key slid into the lock easily and the door opened.

"Oh, thank goodness," she said as she scooted across the front seat to the driver's side and opened the door.

Rory and Eric climbed in beside her. Eric reached out and grabbed the door handle to pull it shut. The door bounced away.

"What happened?" he asked, trying to close the door again.

Mrs. Mueller sat behind the steering wheel and tried to close her door. *Bounce!* The door flew open.

"The locks are frozen," she said.

"How are we going to get to school with both doors flapping?" asked Rory.

The three sat in silence, thinking.

"Rope. Do we have any rope?" asked Rory's mother.

Eric opened the glove compartment and pulled out a long piece of heavy string.

"That will do," she said. "Loop this end through the handle."

Eric pulled the rope through and handed it to Rory, who passed it to her mother. Mrs. Mueller hooked the handle of her door and brought the two ends together.

"Here, Rory, you'll have to hold the rope, since I'll be driving. Whatever you do, don't let go."

"Okay, Mom."

Mrs. Mueller started the engine. It coughed for a minute or two, but then settled to a hum. Backing out the driveway, doors flapping, the windows suddenly fogged up.

"Everybody, stop breathing," laughed Rory's mother as she turned on the defroster.

Eric and Mrs. Mueller cleared away part of the windshield while Rory held tightly onto the rope.

The snow fell more heavily now. The windshield wipers squeaked rhythmically.

"Hey, look," cried Eric.

Jennifer and Margie were walking through drifts of snow on the sidewalk. Rory's mother pulled the car over to the side of the road.

She stuck her head out of the window. "Anyone care for a ride?"

"Great," yelled Margie. "It's cold out here."

"Our heater's out, so I'm afraid it's not much warmer in here," apologized Mrs. Mueller.

Jennifer reached for the back door handle and pulled.

"It's stuck," she said.

"Oh, no," said Rory. "Now what? If they get in the car, we'll have another flapping door."

"And we're out of rope," said Eric.

"Get out of the car, you two," ordered Mrs. Mueller to Rory and Eric.

"Why?" asked Rory.

"Get out so the girls can get in."

Rory groaned but obeyed. *It would have been easier to walk to school,* she thought.

"Our door locks are frozen," Rory explained.

"So if you want a ride, you'll have to climb over the front seat."

"It's too bad my mom had to take her car to the city," said Jennifer.

"Oh, lighten up, Jennifer," said Margie. "This will be fun."

One by one, they climbed over and settled themselves in the back.

Mrs. Mueller wiped off the front seat with an old rag and Rory and Eric slid in. Rory picked up the rope and they were off.

The car rattled as the northwesterly wind blew. Rory shivered as snowflakes plopped onto her nose from above. She glanced behind her. Jennifer looked up to the snow falling from the roof.

"We could have used our umbrellas today," said Rory.

Margie laughed. "I sure know what I'm going to write about today in my journal."

"Somehow, I think Ms. B. may have a different assignment," said Mrs. Mueller.

"What do you mean, Mom?"

"Never mind," she said as she pulled up in front of the school.

As good-byes chorused, Eric and Rory stood to the side. Eric chuckled.

"Why are you laughing?" demanded Rory.

"I'm laughing because you're a lot like your car."

Rory gasped. "Old and broken down?"

"No. Lots of fun."

Rory smiled as they walked to their classroom.

Jennifer was the first one in when Eric opened the door.

"Oh my gosh . . ."

"What?" asked Rory. Her mouth dropped open as she entered the room.

"Will you look at that?" asked Margie.

"I'm looking, I'm looking," said Eric.

"How did it get here?" wondered Margie out loud.

They stared at the large, blown-up picture of complete chaos . . . the dog birthday party.

"I bet your mother did this," said Eric.

Ms. B. smiled. "Today's creative writing assignment will be to write a story that fits the picture."

As Rory took her seat, she turned to Jennifer. "Say, when are you going to invite me for a ride in your Mercedes?"

"Tomorrow?" asked Jennifer, smiling. "But I know it won't be as fun as your two-umbrella car."

About the Author

Elizabeth Koehler-Pentacoff grew up in Wisconsin with a two-umbrella car, a hand-me-down bicycle, and a people-eating couch. Although the car anecdotes really happened, she made up the characters and the rest of the story.

The author of *Louise the One and Only* and *Wish Magic,* Elizabeth currently lives in California with her husband and her son. She has a Yorkshire Terrier who chases big dogs whenever she gets the chance.